Best Stori
Seven-Year-Olds

Enid Blyton
Pictures by Diana Catchpole

Bloomsbury

Enid Blyton titles available at Bloomsbury
Children's Books

Adventure!
Mischief at St Rollo's
The Children of Kidillin
The Secret of Cliff Castle
Smuggler Ben
The Boy Who Wanted a Dog
The Adventure of the Secret Necklace

Happy Days!
The Adventures of Mr Pink-Whistle
Run-About's Holiday
Bimbo and Topsy
Hello Mr Twiddle
Shuffle the Shoemaker
Mr Meddle's Mischief
Snowball the Pony
The Adventures of Binkle and Flip

Enid Blyton Age-Ranged Story Collections
Best Stories for Five-Year-Olds
Best Stories for Six-Year-Olds
Best Stories for Eight-Year-Olds

Contents

Gniel!!

Dear Children

Enid Blyton was my mother and each evening she used to read me her stories. Although many of you read to yourselves now, I hope that someone will read to you if you still enjoy listening to stories.

Sara, one of Enid Blyton's grand-daughters, loved fairy stories best and read all my mother's story books. She wanted to know if fairies and the other little people were real. Perhaps some of you are wondering the same thing.

Long ago, people did not understand the reasons for things that happened – why the cow became ill, why the corn did not grow, why one child was pretty and another plain. So they believed that little creatures who knew powerful magic lived in the world, sometimes helping people but often harming them.

Fairies were tall and beautiful and usually kindly. The mischievous pixies and elves were very small and loved to dance in the moonlight. Brownies were friendly little people and lived to be very old.

Goblins and gnomes were ugly and often very unkind to people. Wizards and witches knew powerful spells and were frightening to fairy folk and humans.

I hope that you will enjoy these stories which are about animals, toys and children as well as fairies and magic.

With love from
Gillian

The Wooden Horse

The wooden horse belonged to Denis. He was a fine little horse, standing on a wooden platform on which small wheels were fixed, so that the horse would run along when he was pulled.

He had a black mane and a black tail of fine hair, and his eyes were very bright and eager, for he was a good and willing little horse, ready to play or to work, just whichever Denis wanted him to do. He was fastened to a small wooden cart, and he could pull this along nicely, for it was not very heavy.

At first Denis liked the little horse and played with him – but then he forgot about him and didn't play with him any more. Worse still, he left the horse and cart out in the garden instead of putting them away properly in the toy cupboard. But he was always doing that – leaving his toys out so that they were scorched by the sun or spoilt by the rain. He was a careless little boy with his toys.

He left the horse and cart at the bottom of the garden by the hedge that grew between his garden and the old field beyond. At first the horse didn't mind, for it was fun to stand and watch the birds hopping about and to see the cat lying warming himself in the sun. But soon he felt cold.

The sun went behind a big cloud and the rain began to pour down. The horse really thought he would be drowned, the rain was so heavy. A big puddle began to form just where he stood and the water came right over his wheels and round his feet. It was horrid.

His tail was soaked and his mane dripped water over his nose. All the paint came off his back, and when the rain stopped, what a funny sight he was! He was very sad, very wet, and very cold.

He stood there all day long, and when the night came he was still there, standing in front of his little cart. Denis had forgotten all about him, that was certain!

The moon came up and lit the garden. The wind was cold and the little horse shivered. Then he sneezed. What a loud sneeze! A-tish-shoo! He looked all round to see if anyone had heard him, and he saw a small brownie-man stopping nearby in surprise. He carried a spade over his shoulder, and wore a workman's apron of brown leather.

'Have you caught cold?' called the brownie, in a gentle voice. 'Shall I put a sack over you to keep you warm?'

'Well, it's too late, I think,' said the wooden horse. 'I stood out in the rain today and got cold then. Denis left me here.'

'He's a horrid boy!' said the brownie crossly. 'He's always leaving his toys out in the rain. I had to rescue a sugar mouse once that was beginning to melt. He doesn't deserve to have toys.'

'What are you working at?' asked the wooden horse, looking at the spade that the brownie was carrying. 'I suppose I couldn't help you. It would make me nice and warm to do a bit of work.'

'Good idea!' cried the brownie, pleased. 'You could help me a lot. I'm building myself a nice house under the hedge nearby, but it takes me a long time to wheel away all the rubbish. If I put it into your cart you could trot away with it and tip it somewhere, couldn't you?'

'Oh, yes!' said the horse eagerly. 'I'd like to do that. But I'm on wheels, you know. I can't walk by myself.'

'Oh, that's easily altered,' said the brownie. He pulled the wheels from the little wooden platform on which the horse stood, and then knocked away the platform from below his feet.

'Now I'll rub a little magic into your legs and you'll be able to trot off just like a real horse!' he said. He rubbed the horse's legs and then the little creature found, to his delight, that he could trot about, using his legs just as real horses do. It was grand!

He followed the brownie to the place where he was building his house. How hard he worked that night! I couldn't tell you how many cartfuls of rubbish he took away and dumped in the old field on the other side of the hedge! The brownie-man was delighted. He had done four times as much work as he usually did in a night. He patted the wooden horse kindly, and gave him a bag of grain to eat. The horse was hungry after his hard work.

'I'm going to take you into the field with me now,' said the brownie. 'You shall lie down and have a good rest. I'll unharness you from the cart. You shall stay near my hole, and if anyone sees you, you must just run down the hole to me and you'll be safe.'

So the wooden horse lay down by the hole where the brownie lived while he was building his house, and slept well. The next night he helped the brownie again and the next. Soon they became great friends. When the house was finished, the brownie began to build another little place beside it, and the horse asked him what it was.

'It's a stable for *you*,' said the brownie-man, beaming all over his kind little face. 'I'm sure Denis doesn't want you, and so you might as well live with me and be my horse – if you'd like to.'

'Oh, I'd love it,' said the horse, overjoyed. 'I'd just love it! I'll work for you each day, and if ever you want to ride anywhere, just tell me, and I'll take you there on my back!'

When everything was finished, the brownie-man went out alone one day and came home proudly carrying four pots of paint – one of brown, one of white, one of red, and the other of blue.

'I'm going to give you another coat of paint,' he said to the delighted wooden horse. 'You look dreadful and so does your cart. Wait till I've finished with you – you'll be smart enough for the king himself!'

He set to work. He painted the horse brown with white spots here and there. He painted

the cart blue with red wheels. You should have seen them when they were finished! They looked lovely.

The brownie-man ran off to wash his hands, telling the horse to stand still in the sun till he was dry. And whilst he was standing there, so smart and fine, who should come by but Denis himself!

When he saw the wooden horse and cart, he stared at it in surprise. Could it be *his* horse and cart? What had happened? How smart they looked! Look at those fine red wheels! Oh, he must take this toy to the nursery and play with it!

The little horse was filled with horror when he saw Denis – and when the little boy came towards him to take him away, he neighed in a high voice.

'Help! Help!'

In a trice the brownie-man rushed out of the hedge and ran up to him. He jumped into the cart, took up the reins and said: 'Gee-up!'

Before Denis could do anything the horse galloped off at top speed, and the cart with the brownie in it bumped and rattled over the grass.

'Hi! Hi!' shouted Denis. 'That's *my* horse

and cart! Come back!'

But they didn't come back! Denis never saw them again, but he thought about them a great deal.

'I must have left the horse and cart out in the rain,' he thought at last. 'So the brownie took them for his own. Well, it serves me right. I'll look after my toys better. I'm not going to have that brownie taking them all for himself!'

He did look after his toys better – but all the same, he didn't get his horse and cart back! No, the wooden horse is still with the brownie-man, and they are very well known in Fairyland indeed. You can see them in the streets there any day.

A Surprise for
Mother Hubbard

Mother Hubbard was very poor. She often opened her cupboard door and found that every shelf inside was empty. She scrubbed Dame Heyho's floor three times a week, and for that she had a pound a time, but three pounds didn't go very far when there were so many things to buy.

Paddy-paws was Mother Hubbard's dog. He was very fond of Mother Hubbard, and was very sorry she was so poor. He would have liked to get her nice things to eat, a warm shawl to wear, and a nice big arm-chair. But he hadn't a penny of his own, so the most he could do was to eat as few dog biscuits as possible to save Mother Hubbard buying many. If he felt dreadfully hungry he would go and catch himself a rat.

Now one day a great adventure happened to Paddy-paws when he was out shopping. Every day he took a basket, which he cleverly carried by the handle in his mouth, and went to shop for Mother Hubbard. She always used to put a note in the bottom of the basket to tell the shopman what she wanted.

This morning she had put a note in for the baker. She wanted a small loaf of stale bread.

'Go to the baker's, Paddy-paws,' she said, and put the handle of the basket into his mouth. He wagged his tail and set off. He went to the baker's and the man read the note. He wrapped up a small loaf in a piece of paper and put it into the basket. Then Paddy-paws set off home again.

Now, on the way he passed the Witch High-hat. She was hurrying down the road, holding a box very tightly in her hand. She kept looking behind her as she went and Paddy-paws wondered why.

When she saw Paddy-paws she ran up to him and petted him, a thing she had never done before.

'Good dog,' she said. 'Will you carry this box for me a little while? Thank you.'

She slipped the box into the basket on top of the bread. Paddy-paws was surprised and didn't know what to do. The witch walked along the road, humming. Suddenly there came the sound of running feet behind them, and Paddy-paws turned and saw Wise-one the Wizard running down the road, with a police-man on each side of him.

'Stop thief! Stop thief!' he yelled. 'Here you are, policeman! Take her to prison! She's stolen one of my best spells!'

The policeman caught hold of the witch and searched her from head to foot – but they could find no spell. They shook their heads at the wizard.

'She hasn't got it,' they said. 'We can't take her to prison, Wise-one.'

Paddy-paws was frightened when he saw the policeman. He ran off as fast as his legs could carry him. He though the policemen might take him to prison too, because he had been walking beside the witch.

He tore home to Mother Hubbard. She was out, so he carefully put the basket down in the corner of the kitchen as she had taught him to do. He forgot all about the little box in it. Then he felt very hungry, so he ran out to see if the next-door cat would let him share her dish of bread and milk.

Mother Hubbard had gone to scrub Dame Heyho's floor. On the way back she passed the police-station. Outside was a big notice. She stopped to read it. This is what it said:

'LOST OR STOLEN. A red box with a powerful spell inside. Anyone returning it to Wise-one the Wizard will receive one hundred pieces of gold.'

'Ooh!' said Mother Hubbard longingly. 'How I wish *I* could find that! But I never get any luck at all.'

She went home, tired and hungry. She hoped that Paddy-paws had got the loaf of bread for her. He was a good little dog, and she did wish her cupboard wasn't always so bare. She would like to give him a fat, juicy bone.

She saw the basket in the corner of the kitchen, and she went to get the bread from it. She saw a red box on top of the bread, and she wondered what it was. She took it up and opened it. Inside was a strange yellow powder, mixed with tiny blue balls. It had a curious smell.

Mother Hubbard smelt it – and at once she knew what it was. It was a spell to make people as big as ever they liked – as big as the biggest giant in the world, or bigger! It was a very powerful spell indeed.

'My goodness me, wherever did this come from? What a strange thing!' said Mother Hubbard to herself. 'Paddy-paws, Paddy-paws! How did this come into the basket?'

Paddy-paws rushed in from the garden. He jumped up at Mother Hubbard and licked her hand.

'Old Witch High-hat popped it into my basket this morning,' he said. 'I don't think it belonged to her, so I brought it home to you. What is it?'

'It's the powerful spell that Wise-one the Wizard lost!' said Mother Hubbard joyfully.

'I expect the witch stole it, and when she saw people after her, she popped it into your basket, hoping to take it out again when she could. It's a good thing she didn't come round here this morning while I was out. She could easily have taken it out of the basket!'

Mother Hubbard slipped the little red box into her bag. She started out to go to the wizard, and then she suddenly stopped.

'Wait a minute,' she said. 'I might meet the witch, and if she thought I was going to the wizard she might put a spell on me and turn me into a black beetle or something. Where's that red box I had those sugar biscuits in? It's exactly like this red box with the spell inside. Look, Paddy-paws, I'll put the biscuit box into your basket and you shall come with me and carry it. Then if we meet the witch she will take the red box out of your basket and go off without harming me – and I shall have the right box all the time!'

She slipped the old biscuit box into the basket and Paddy-paws took it up by the handle once more. Then he and Mother Hubbard set off.

Witch High-hat came round the corner just as they went down the street. She had been watching for them. She hurried up to Mother Hubbard.

'I gave your dog a box to carry for me this morning,' she said fiercely. 'He ran away with it. Where is it? Give it to me or I'll turn you into a frog!'

Mother Hubbard and Paddy-paws pretended to be very frightened. Paddy-paws dropped the basket and the old red biscuit box rolled out of it. The witch saw it, pounced on it, and she ran off crying: 'Oh, I've got it, after all!'

Then Mother Hubbard and Paddy-paws

chuckled quietly to themselves and hurried on to Wise-one's house. He was delighted to see them and when he heard the tale of how they had deceived the wicked witch, he laughed till the tears ran down his long beard.

'Yes, that's the spell I lost,' he said, opening the red box. 'If that old witch had got hold of it, she would have used it and made herself the biggest giantess in the world. And then goodness knows what mischief she would have done! Here is your bag of a hundred pieces of gold, Mother Hubbard. I hope you will spend it well!'

She did! She bought a new rocking-chair for herself, a fine red shawl and a new bonnet. And for Paddy-paws she bought a big bone every day from the butcher – and now when she opens her cupboard, it is no longer bare, but full of the loveliest things to eat. Paddy-paws *is* pleased!

A Real Game of Hide-and-seek

It all happened because of a game of hide-and-seek. Jim, Dickie, and Martha had gone to the woods to play, and they each chose a game. First they played policemen and burglars, then they played schools, and last of all Dickie wanted hide-and-seek.

'You hide your eyes, Dickie,' said Jim, 'and Martha and I will hide ourselves. I know a lovely place. You'll never be able to find us!'

So Dickie went behind a blackberry bush and hid his eyes while he counted a hundred, very slowly. Jim took Martha's hand and pulled her towards an old oak tree that grew some distance away.

'I've found a lovely hiding-place!' he whispered. 'I climbed a little way up that oak tree the other day and there's an enormous hole inside it. I thought we'd get into the hollow, and I'm sure Dickie will never find us!'

Martha skipped in excitement. What fun to get right inside a tree! They soon reached the oak. It was a big tree, very old indeed.

'I'll give you a push up,' said Jim to Martha. 'Hurry now, or Dickie will be coming.'

Martha climbed a little way up the old tree, with Jim behind her. She soon saw the big hole and let herself down into it. To her surprise the big tree was quite hollow inside and there was plenty of room for them both to stand up there.

'Sh! Dickie's coming!' said Martha suddenly.

'He can't be coming so soon,' said Jim. 'He always counts his hundred very slowly.'

'Well, I can hear *someone*!' said Martha. So she could – but it wasn't Dickie! The children heard two people coming, and by the sound of their voices they were men. They were talking in low voices as if they didn't want to be overheard.

'Anyone about here this afternoon?' said one man.

'One or two kids, that's all,' said the other. 'We'll soon frighten them off if they come near here.'

Martha felt rather frightened already. Jim was afraid she was going to cry, and he took her hand and squeezed it.

'Don't make a sound!' he whispered in her ear. The little girl nodded bravely.

'Is this the tree?' said one of the men, still in a very low voice. If they hadn't been just inside the tree the children would never have heard what was being said.

'Yes,' said the other. 'Here, give me the bag. I'll put it into the hole. Nobody's about, and it's as safe a hiding-place as I know! The police will have to play a good game of hide-and-seek if they find it

here! Nobody knows this place but me.'

There was the sound of someone scrambling up the old trunk. Then a big bag was let down into the hollow and was pressed down between the two scared children. They made no sound but made room for the heavy bag, glad that it hadn't been put on their heads.

'That's done!' said the man, jumping down. 'Come on, let's get away now. I don't want anyone to see us in the woods.'

The children heard the sound of running feet, but for a long time they stayed still. Then they heard Dickie's voice quite near, calling, 'Oh, I give up, Martha and Jim! I've hunted and hunted and can't find you. Come out, wherever you are!'

'Dickie! Dickie!' called Jim. 'Is anyone about in the woods?'

'Not now!' called Dickie. 'There were two men, but they've gone. Where are you? Do come out!'

Then Jim climbed out of the hollow tree and pulled Martha up too. Then he reached down for the bag and dragged it up. Dickie ran to them shouting: 'So that's where you were! What a clever place! But I say, Jim, what's that bag?'

Ah, what was it indeed? When Jim opened it he shouted in surprise. For inside there were many brown leather boxes, some small and some big, and when they were opened, guess what was in them!

There were necklaces, bracelets, brooches, rings – the loveliest things that the children had ever seen. They stared at them, and then they looked excitedly at each other.

'They're the things that were stolen from Mr Harris, the jeweller, on Tuesday!' cried Jim. 'I say what a find! Let's carry them to the police station! Help me, Dickie. The bag's too heavy for one to carry.'

The three excited children carried the heavy bag to the town, and went straight to the police station. You should have seen how amazed the policemen were when they opened the bag and heard the children's story!

'So the men are going back to the tree tonight, are they?' said a big burly policeman. 'Well, they won't find there what they expect! I'll take three of my men and we'll lie in wait for the thieves. What a surprise for them! It was very lucky that you happened to be playing hide-and-seek there this afternoon, children!'

The two thieves were caught that night and well punished. All the lovely jewels were taken back to Mr Harris by the police, and he was surprised and pleased.

The children were delighted with their adventure – but it wasn't *quite* ended. Mr Harris was so pleased to get back all his goods that he sent three small parcels to the children – and what do you suppose was inside them?

In each parcel was a lovely silver watch, ticking away merrily, and a note was there, too. It said: 'Hoping you will have lots more games of hide-and-seek, and be as lucky as you were last time!' Wasn't it kind of Mr Harris?

The Tale of Tibbles

Tibbles was a tabby cat. She wasn't very big, but she had fine whiskers, kind green eyes, and a very loud purr. She belonged to Mary and John, and they loved her very much.

They loved her kittens too, but Mother didn't like them. She said it was so hard to find enough people to give them to.

'Well, why can't we keep them all?' said Mary. 'I'd love to have Tibbles's kittens.'

'Don't be silly, Mary,' said Mother. 'Why, if we kept all Tibbles's kittens, we should have nothing to eat ourselves! They would eat us out of house and home! Tibbles has had about twenty kittens already. I really think we shall have to give her away to someone – I know she is a good mouser, but really, I don't know anyone to give her kittens to now. All our friends have a kitten belonging to her.'

'Give Tibbles away!' cried Mary and John, quite shocked. 'Oh, Mother! You *couldn't*! Why, she's ours, and she loves us.'

'Well, I shall have to take her next kittens to the vet, then,' said Mother. Mary and John ran off, tears in their eyes. Take the dear little kittens that Tibbles gave them to the vet? It would be dreadful!

'Let's go and find Tibbles and tell her to be sure to hide her kittens next time,' said Mary. 'If she puts them in her basket, as she usually does, Mother will find them – and I couldn't bear them to be taken to the vet, could you, John?'

Tibbles was fast asleep on the old wall outside, warm in the sunshine. John woke her and told her to be sure and hide her next kittens away safely somewhere. Tibbles stretched out her grey paws, listened, and purred. She was very fond of Mary and John.

The children lived in an old thatched cottage. It had belonged to their grandfather and to his father, too. It was a funny house inside – you had to go down steps into some rooms and up steps into others. The windows were latticed, like the windows of fairy cottages. The house was very, very old, and Mother had often told them about a buried treasure that was supposed to be there.

'It is in the garden somewhere,' she said. 'Your great-great-grandfather buried it there, so it is said – but no one has ever found it, so I think it is just a tale!'

The children believed in that buried treasure and, dear me, how they dug and dug to find it! But although they found all sorts of funny things – bones the dog had buried, broken pieces of long-ago china, and once an old heavy penny – they had never found the treasure!

About once a week they dug in the garden to see if they could find it – and one day, when they were digging busily, not long after they had warned Tibby about her kittens, they heard her mewing to them. They ran to her – and she took them into the kitchen.

And, would you believe it, in her basket by the fire were five little new kittens!

'Oh, Tibbles, we told you to hide them and not put them in your basket!' cried John. 'Now

Mother will see them and you'll have them taken away!'

Mother did see them – and she shook her head at Tibbles. 'I'm sorry, puss-cat,' she said, 'but I don't know anyone who will have your kittens this time. I must give them to the gardener next door, and he will have to take them to the vet.'

The next-door gardener came to have a look at them, and he put them into a basket to take away. Mary and John cried bitterly, and as for poor Tibbles, she went nearly mad with rage.

The gardener went off next door, carrying the basket. He put it down by the shed while he went to fetch his tools. Tibbles was following him – and as soon as she saw the basket laid down, and the gardener gone, she ran to her kittens.

Quietly she lifted them out, one by one, and

took them to a bush. She laid them there in a heap and told them to be quiet. Presently the gardener came back – and when he found no kittens in his basket he was most astonished!

'Now where have they gone?' he wondered. 'They were too small to have crawled away by themselves! Someone must have taken them out!'

He went back to the thatched cottage next door and asked the children's mother if she had the kittens. But she hadn't of course! John and Mary listened in surprise. They looked at one another, both quite certain that Tibbles must have found her kittens and taken them out of the basket to hide them!

'Well, never mind,' said their mother to the gardener. 'I expect Tibbles will bring them back to her own basket soon – you can fetch them at tea time.'

But Tibbles didn't take her five kittens back to her basket. No, she was far wiser than that! She waited with them under the bush until it was nearly dark, and then, carrying her kittens one by one by the scruff of their necks, she found a new hiding place for them. She had known it for a long time, and had often slept there herself, when she had been out late at night and had found the kitchen door locked when she wanted to get in.

Up by the biggest chimney stack was a hole. It went right down into the thatch, where it widened out into a place quite big enough to hold a cat and kittens. It was quite dry, and very warm, for the straw held the heat. Sometimes a fieldmouse ran up into the thatch and found its way down to the hole – and if Tibbles was there, it never came out again! Tibbles and the mice were the only ones who knew of that chimney stack hole.

Tibbles climbed up the roof to the hole five times with a kitten in her mouth each time. She knew she would be safe there. She was angry and afraid because for the first time someone had dared to take her precious kittens away from her. She was not even going to show Mary and John where they were this time!

When Tibbles's basket was found empty in the morning – no cat there, and no kittens either – mother was surprised.

'Tibbles has hidden her kittens somewhere,' she said. 'I wonder where. You had better look under the privet hedge and under the bushes, children. Or she might have hidden them in the woodshed. Go and look there.'

The children went. They had to do as they were told, but they hoped they wouldn't find the kittens. Of course they couldn't see them anywhere, and they didn't see Tibbles either! She was snug in the thatch with her blind kittens, much too wise to come when she was called, for she was not going to give away her hiding place!

When it was almost dark she slipped down the roof and stole into the kitchen. She found her plate of fish and milk and ate it all up hungrily.

'Here's Tibbles, Mother!' cried John, pleased to see the little tabby.

'Watch to see where she goes, John,' said Mother, 'and then we shall see where she has hidden her kittens.'

John watched. Tibbles knew he was watching. *She* wasn't going to show him where her kittens were by jumping straight up on to the rain barrel and from there to the roof, which was the way she usually went to her hiding place. She trotted out to the garden, disappeared under the thick privet hedge, crept through a ditch of nettles on the other side, back to the house by another way, and, while everyone was hunting under the hedge, she quietly leapt on to the rain barrel, climbed up the thatch roof, and went back unseen to her five kittens. Ah, Tibbles was a clever and wise little cat, there was no doubt of that!

Of course, not a single kitten was found under the privet hedge, when John, Mary, and Mother looked there again.

'Tibbles must have put her kittens out in the field,' said Mother at last. 'Well, come along in now – it's too dark to see.'

Three weeks went by, and still no one had found

Tibbles's kittens. They were no longer blind now. They had all opened their blue eyes and were staring round at the hole which was their home. They had little mewing voices, and they were always wiggling about in their cosy hole. Tibbles was very proud of them. They were the prettiest kittens she had ever had. Their coats were beautiful, and their whiskers were growing long. Soon they were able to crawl about in the hole. They grew strong. They played with one another, rolling over and over, mewing loudly. And then, one day, the biggest kitten of all thought it would like to follow its mother out of the hole and see where she went!

But its legs were too weak to climb after her. It waited until its legs were much stronger, and then it tried again. Up it climbed and up – and at last reached the small hole by the chimney stack through which Tibbles went in and out. It crawled through it, and there it was, on the sunny thatched roof, blinking its blue eyes in the strong light!

It was frightened and mewed loudly for its mother. Tibbles was hunting for mice in the fields, but she heard that frightened cry. Back she raced, rushed through the hedge, jumped up on the rain barrel, and ran up the roof to her kitten.

And Mary and John saw her! They looked up in astonishment at seeing Tibbles climbing up the thatch – and there, by the chimney, they saw a tiny kitten, mewing loudly! Tibbles picked it up by the neck, squeezed herself through the hole, and disappeared.

'Did you see, Mary?' cried John, in excitement. 'That's where Tibbles is hiding her kittens – in a hole in the thatch, just by the chimney stack. Fancy that! How clever of her!'

Mother was out, so they couldn't tell her. They longed to see the kittens, and they couldn't wait till Mother came home. What could they do?

'I know!' said John. 'We'll get the ladder from the yard, and put it up against the thatched roof. It's so slanting that it will be quite safe and not too steep for us to climb up. Come on, Mary, help me!'

Off they went to the yard. There was a long ladder there, and it was heavy. But the two children were strong and between them they managed to carry it to the house. They leaned it on the roof, and it rested on the thatch quite safely.

'I'll go up first,' said John. 'Hold the ladder for me, Mary.'

So Mary held the ladder, and up went John, step by step. He came to the chimney and saw the little hole down which Tibbles had gone. He put in his hand and felt about. Yes – the kittens were there – and so was Tibbles. She hissed at John, but she did not scratch him.

'Come up now, and feel in the hole,' said John to Mary, climbing down. 'There's quite a big place in the roof just there.'

So up went Mary. She put her arm into the hold and felt the kittens too. She pulled one out – and cried out to see what a beauty it was. She put it back again, and once more felt round the big hole inside to find another kitten.

But this time she felt something round and hard. She felt round it with her hand. What could it be? She pulled at it, but it was too heavy to move.

She pulled again – and this time she heard a sound – just a little chinky sound. Mary's eyes grew wide, and she almost fell off the ladder in excitement. It had sounded like money!

'John, John!' she shouted. 'There's something in this hole – something that feels like a big leather bag of money. I heard it chink! It's too heavy for me to move!'

'It must be the treasure!' shouted John, jumping up and down in excitement. 'Come down, Mary, quick, and let me feel!'

'No, you come up too,' said Mary. 'We can both hold on to the ladder and feel.'

So up went John too, and he felt the round bag of money, but he couldn't move it at all, it was so heavy. Just as the two children were struggling to get it, they heard a voice from down below – an angry and frightened voice.

'Children! What *are* you doing? It is most dangerous to be up there like that! Come down at once. I am very cross with you!'

It was their mother!

John and Mary looked round, their faces red, their eyes bright.

'Mother! Mother! We've found the buried treasure – only it's not buried, it's hidden up here, in a hole in the thatch!'

'Please come down,' said Mother, still very worried in case they should fall. 'Come down at once, and then I will listen to you.'

'But Mother . . .' began John, who couldn't bear to leave the treasure.

'AT ONCE!' said mother, in a voice that had to be obeyed. Both children climbed down carefully. At first Mother was too frightened and too angry with them to listen, but when she saw that neither child was hurt, she heard their story in amazement.

'You must be mistaken,' she said at last. 'I don't expect there's anything of the sort up there. Look – here's Daddy. We'll tell him and he can go up and see.'

It wasn't long before Daddy was up that ladder. He put his hand in the hole and Tibbles scratched him and spat. But Daddy didn't mind. His hand closed over the round

bag, and he tugged. It certainly *was* heavy. But Daddy was strong and he pulled the leather bag to the hole. He heaved it up and out it came, a brown bag whose leather was still as good as new!

'It's full of some sort of money!' called Daddy. 'My goodness, it's heavy!'

He climbed down and Mother and the children crowded round him. Daddy put the big, heavy bag on the grass and undid the leather thongs that did up the neck of the bag. It came open – and out fell scores and scores of coins, all gold!

'My great-great-grandfather's hoard!' said Daddy. 'So he didn't bury it in the garden after all! No wonder we couldn't find it there!'

What excitement there was that night! There were five hundred pounds in the leather bag, all in golden sovereigns, and Daddy and Mother soon began to plan what they could do with it!

Everyone forgot about Tibbles and her kittens. Tibbles lay in her hole, trembling. Her hiding place was found. What would happen to her kittens? Would they be taken away again? Tibbles was sad and frightened. She licked her kittens again and again and cuddled them close to her.

The next day Mary thought of Tibbles. She had not been down to get her breakfast from the bowl. Mary wondered why – and then she guessed. Poor Tibbles was frightened, of course!

Mary rushed to Mother at once.

'Mother! Mother! We've forgotten about Tibbles! Oh, Mother, please can we keep her kittens this time? After all, if it hadn't been for Tibbles being clever enough to find that hole we would never have found Great-great-grandfather's money! So Tibbles has done us a very good turn!'

'Of course poor old Tibbles can keep her kittens,' said Mother. 'They are much too old to take from her now until we find new homes for them.'

So Daddy went up the ladder again, and brought down Tibbles's kittens one by one. They were beautiful kittens, with the loveliest thick coats, fine eyes, and long whiskers.

'Why, Mother!' said Daddy. 'These are lovely kittens! We shan't have any difficulty about giving *these* away! They're the nicest ones Tibbles has ever had!'

The next day all the newspapers printed the story of how Tibbles had found a bag of treasure through hiding her kittens in a hole –

and dozens of people came to see the little grey cat and to admire her beautiful kittens.

'Would you sell me one of the kittens?' said first one person and then another. 'I will pay you ten pounds. I should be proud to have a kitten belonging to such a clever mother!'

Fancy that! All Tibbles's kittens went to good homes when they were big enough. Tibbles kept them while they were small, so she was very happy. She didn't want them when they grew big, for she knew that they must go to other homes and catch mice for grown-ups. She only wanted them while they were little, so that she could love them and take care of them.

Mother let John and Mary have the money that people gave them for the kittens.

'That's only fair!' she said. 'Tibbles is your cat, and if the kittens can be sold, then you must have the money to spend as you like. Tibbles found Daddy and me that big bag of money and we feel very rich now. What shall you spend *your* money on?'

'I'm going to buy a fine new basket and a cushion for dear old Tibbles, first of all!' said Mary.

'And I'm going to buy her a big tin of sardines,' said John. Wasn't it nice of them?

Tibbles still lives with them, a fat little grey tabby, happy and contented. I've got one of her kittens, so that's how I know this story!

White Trousers

The teddy bear in Jack's playroom was a fine-looking fellow. He wore a red jersey, a little blue scarf, and white trousers. At least, they were white when they were new, but now they were rather dirty.

He was very proud of his clothes. 'You see, only the *Best* Bears have clothes,' he told everyone. 'Some poor bears have no clothes at all, only their fur. But I've very nice clothes, haven't I?'

'Yes. So you must be one of the Best Bears!' said Angelina, the biggest doll, with a laugh. 'Come here, Teddy. You've a button off your coat! Now, the very Best Bears never have buttons off, you know.'

'Oh, dear!' said the bear, in alarm, squinting down at his coat with his big glass eyes. 'Yes, there's a button gone. Could you sew it on, please, Angelina? You really are so good with a needle.'

Angelina found the button and sewed it on. The bear gave her a furry kiss.

'Ooooh,' she said, 'your whiskers tickle me! There! You're a nice little bear, and certainly one of the best, because you're always kind and jolly!'

All the toys loved the little bear. They belonged to Jack, a noisy, untidy boy who liked his toys but didn't bother much about them. If one broke he didn't mend it but threw it away. The toys didn't like that. They thought they should be mended if they broke, and so they should, of course.

One day something happened. It was a rainy day and Jack had to be indoors. So he found his paints and his painting book, and filled a jar with water. He stuck his paintbrush into it and then rubbed it on one of his paints. He looked round at his toys.

'I think I'll draw one of you and paint your picture,' he said. 'Now, who shall it be? I think

I'll have *you*, Teddy – you'll be easy to draw!'

He picked up the teddy bear and put him on the table, standing up straight. The bear was very proud and pleased. Ah, now he would have his picture painted and he would be famous!

Mother put her head round the door. 'Oh, Jack – I see you're using your paints. Please be careful of that tablecloth. I told you to take it off if you want to do anything messy.'

'Oh, Mother, I won't spill anything. I'll be careful!' said Jack, impatiently.

He drew the little bear, white trousers and all. Then he picked up his paintbrush again, rubbed it on this paint and that, and began to splash the colours on to the paper. How the bear wished he could see the picture! And then Jack moved his hand too quickly and knocked the jar of painting water over on the tablecloth!

'Bother!' said Jack, staring at the coloured pool of water. 'I must wipe it up before Mother comes in. But what with?'

There was no cloth or duster to be seen. Jack could hear his mother in the next room, and he looked wildly round for something to wipe up the mess. He suddenly grabbed the bear.

'I'll have your white trousers!' he said. And, oh dear, he tore them off the surprised little bear! He mopped up the pool of water with the thick trousers, and then covered the wet patch with his painting book. Now Mother wouldn't know!

The bear was full of dismay. His trousers, his lovely white trousers! They had been used to mop up that water – and oh, goodness gracious, Jack had now thrown them into the fire! They burned slowly for they were damp. The bear sat down suddenly on the table, feeling quite ill.

When Jack had gone down to his tea the bear climbed down miserably. The toys clustered round him, sorry for him.

'You look peculiar,' said the toy soldier. 'Hadn't you better take off your coat and tie? It looks odd to wear those and no trousers.'

'No, no. Let me keep my coat and tie,' said the bear, holding on to them as if he thought the toys were going to take them off. 'Oh, dear – my nice white trousers! Jack threw them in the fire, all wet and messy – and they've *burrrrnnnnt!*'

He began to cry. The toys tried to comfort him.

'It's a shame,' said the pink cat. 'He must feel cold without his white trousers.'

'Oh, I do, I do,' wept the bear. 'And I'm not one of the Best Bears any more because I'm only half-dressed. I shall never be happy again!'

'It was mean of Jack,' said Angelina, beginning to think hard. 'He's a naughty boy. He does lots of things that his mother doesn't guess. For instance, she thinks he cleans his teeth night and morning and washes his neck and behind his ears with his face flannel. But he doesn't.'

'He *never* uses his flannel!' said the toy

soldier. 'He only just splashes water on his face.'

Angelina suddenly looked at the soldier. 'I've an idea,' she said. 'Quite a good one. Why shouldn't we get Jack's white face flannel and make the bear a pair of white trousers out of it? Jack never uses it, so it won't matter!'

'Oh, Angelina, please, please do!' begged the bear and kissed her so that his whiskers tickled her again. 'Oh, Angelina, you're the cleverest doll in the world!'

Angelina laughed. She sent the toy soldier to climb up to Jack's basin and fetch the white flannel. It was quite dry because Jack never used it. He put it down beside Angelina. She took the pair of scissors that Jack used to cut his nails, and she began to cut the flannel!

All the toys watched her. How clever Angelina was! Snip, snip, snip, snippety, snip!

'There's one leg,' said Angelina, 'and there's another. And this bit is to go round his tummy, and that is for his back. My, bear, you're going to look fine!'

It really was exciting to see Angelina make those white trousers. She sewed away with her needle, she sent the toy soldier to get a button from Mother's workbasket, and she made a nice buttonhole, so that the white trousers could fasten tightly.

'There!' she said. 'They're finished. Try them on, Teddy dear!'

So the bear tried them on, putting first one fat leg into them and then the other. He pulled them up and buttoned them. Then he walked proudly about in front of the toys.

'Perfect!' said the soldier.

'They fit him beautifully!' said the pink cat. 'I wouldn't mind a pair like that myself, though I suppose I'd have to have two pairs for my four legs.'

'You look sweet, Teddy,' said Angelina, laughing. 'Face-flannel trousers! Who would have thought they could look so fine? You certainly are one of the Best Bears again now!'

'What *I*'m wondering,' said the toy soldier, 'what *I*'m wondering is – what will Jack say when his mother asks him how he manages to wash himself properly without his face flannel?'

'He'll have to own up for once!' said Angelina. 'He'll have to say it's disappeared and he hasn't *been* washing himself!'

'Oh, I'm so happy!' sang the little bear, walking up and down. 'Look at my white trousers, everyone, do look!'

So they looked – and I'd have liked to look, too. Face-flannel trousers – well, well, well!

The Swallow that was Left Behind

There was once a young swallow that had a very happy time in our land all through the summer. When the cold days came the old swallows called him.

'Little-wings, you must come with us,' they said. 'We are gathering together ready to fly from here to a warm country far away.'

'But I don't want to go away from here!' cried Little-wings. 'Let me stay a little longer.'

'No,' said the old birds. 'You must come. Soon there will be no insects for you to eat here, and you will starve if you stay.'

'How do you know?' asked Little-wings, rudely. 'If you never stay for the winter, you don't know what it is like, do you? The freck-led thrush stays, and the little robin. Why can't I stay too?'

'Because swallows never do,' answered the old birds patiently. 'Come with us, and do as you're told.'

Little-wings thought he knew better. He didn't want to fly from the land he knew; far away over the sea to a strange country.

'I should get very tired,' he said to himself. 'I shall stay here. I will hide myself away till all the rest have gone.'

He found a thick ivy-grown wall, and hid under the leaves. He watched all the swallows gathering together on the telegraph wires and on the roof of the old barn. There were hundreds of them, twittering excitedly. They knew that it was time to go, for the cold north wind was blowing strongly. Little-wings heard them talking, and laughed to think that they would go without him.

One evening they flew. Every swallow rose in the air, and flew steadily southwards to where the sea gleamed blue. The strong north wind blew behind them, and soon they were out of sight. Little-wings was the only swallow left in England.

The next few days were sunny and warm, and Little-wings enjoyed himself very much. He made friends with a robin, and caught quite a lot of flies that danced in the sunshine. But the nights were cold, and Little-wings shivered, and wished he had a few more feathers.

When November came the days were foggy and wet. Little-wings found that flies were getting fewer and fewer. The robin didn't want him and drove him away.

'There are not enough insects for you in this garden,' said he. 'Go somewhere else.'

But wherever he went there seemed to be a robin who said the same thing.

'In the winter we each take a beat of our own,' said one. 'We don't allow anyone else there, for then there would not be enough food. Go away!'

Little-wings was cold, lonely, and hungry. How he wished he had gone with the other swallows when he had the chance!

'I was young and foolish,' he thought. 'Oh, what shall I do? I shall soon die of cold, and when the others come back in the warm springtime I shall not be here to greet them!'

When snow and frost came the little swallow was nearly frozen. He was only skin and bone, for he had had nothing to eat for days. There were no flies to be found at all. Even the

robins had to go and beg for crumbs at back doors.

He sat huddled up on a frosty post, feeling very cold and ill. Suddenly he heard a voice nearby.

'Why, look! Here's a little swallow! It didn't fly off with the others in the autumn! Oh, Mummy, poor little thing, it's nothing but skin and feathers! Let's take it home and put it with our other birds.'

Then Little-wings felt himself gently picked up and carried into a warm house. He was put into a great big cage where many other little birds flew and chirruped gaily. They were foreign ones, and Little-wings did not understand their language, but he knew they were friendly.

The little girl who had rescued him gave him food. It was warm in the cage, and soon the little swallow felt better. In a day or two he was flying about merrily with the others, thankful that he was not in the cold world outside.

There he stayed, happy and well-cared for till the warm spring days came. Then the little girl took him from the cage and set him free.

'Your brothers and sisters will soon be back!'

she cried. 'Go and welcome them.'

He flew off into the sunshine, and that very day the first swallows came back to England. They were tired after their long journey, and Little-wings gave them a warm welcome. He told them how foolish he had been, and how the little girl had rescued him.

'We'll all build in the barn near her house this year!' cried the swallows. 'And you'll be sure to come with us when we fly away again next time, won't you, Little-wings?'

'I will! I will!' cried the swallow, and off he went to tell the little girl that summer had come.

The Pinned-on Tail

The pink monkey had a very long tail –
but do you know he had to keep it
pinned on because it was loose and fell
off if he didn't.

Poor monkey! He was very sad about this.
You see, he was a grand monkey indeed, bright
pink, with a brown nose, green eyes and paws
very like hands – but his pinned-on tail spoilt
him.

But what was he to do about it? He didn't
want it sewn on, because he felt sure it would
hurt him. He did once borrow some glue and
try to stick it on – but unfortunately he got
the glue all over himself, and stuck *both* ends

of his tail on – one to his back and the other to his front – so that was worse than ever.

He also sat down on a piece of newspaper whilst he was trying to glue himself, and when he got up, he had stuck to the paper – so for a long time he had to walk about with sheets of paper behind him. Everyone laughed till they cried – and then the teddy bear kindly offered to try to get it off.

It hurt a bit – but at last the monkey was quite free of all the newspaper. The teddy bear wrapped it up and was just going to throw it into the fire when the monkey gave a scream.

'Teddy! You've pulled my tail away too – don't throw it into the fire!'

The teddy opened the newspaper – and there was the tail, all screwed up too! The monkey pounced on it and took it.

'Ooh! It nearly went into the fire. Teddy, where is there a safety pin? An ordinary pin is no use.'

Teddy went to Nurse's workbasket and took out a big safety pin. The monkey screwed himself round and pinned on his long woolly tail. He wouldn't let the teddy do it in case it hurt him.

'It's crooked,' said Teddy.

'Tisn't,' said the monkey, trying to look over his shoulder at his tail.

'Tis!' said the teddy.

'Well, I *like* it crooked,' said the monkey. But he didn't like it crooked. He didn't like it pinned on at all. It did spoil his beauty so. He looked quite all right from the front – but from behind he looked dreadful – all safety pin and crooked tail.

One night he thought he would creep out and go to the little old woman who lived under the hedge nearby. People said she was very clever. The monkey felt sure she was clever enough to fix his tail on without glue or pins.

So off he went. The moon shone down on his safety pin and made it very bright. He hunted about for the little old woman, but he couldn't seem to find her house.

Then suddenly he heard a shout for help.

'Quick! Help me! Help me!'

Monkey ran on all fours to the place where the shouting came from. He was just in time to see a small elf getting up off the ground – and a frog hopping away fast with something in his front paws.

'What's the matter?' asked the monkey.

'Oh, that horrid, horrid frog has stolen my

lovely shawl,' sobbed the elf. 'I shall get cold! I'm going to a party, and I shall get so hot dancing – and then I shall get a chill afterwards. I always do if I have no scarf or shawl. Oh, I'm so sad!'

'Can't you go home and borrow a scarf?' said the monkey feeling sorry for the pretty little elf.

'My home is ever so far away,' said the elf, drying her eyes and looking at the monkey.

Then she saw his long woolly tail, which he had curled round his waist for the moment. She pointed to it.

'Oh, Monkey! If you'd lend me that lovely woolly thing you've got round your waist I could wrap it round my throat and use it for a scarf. Then I wouldn't get cold.'

'But that's my *tail*,' said the monkey, offended.

'Oh, is it?' said the elf. 'Why don't you let it go loose then? It seems funny to tie it round your waist.'

'Well, I tie it round because it's only pinned on,' said the monkey. 'And you see, if the pin came undone I might lose my tail and not know it.'

'Only *pinned* on!' shrieked the elf. 'Well, unpin it then and lend it to me, can't you? It would make such a LOVELY scarf. Oh dear, darling, beautiful Monkey, unpin your tail and lend it to me, do, do, do!'

The elf flung her arms round the surprised monkey – and she was so little and so sweet and so loving that he simply couldn't say no to her. So he solemnly unpinned his tail, took it off and handed it to her. The elf wrapped it round her neck and danced in delight. 'It's warm, warm, warm!' she sang. 'Come on, Monkey darling – come with me to the party!'

And, to the pink monkey's great astonishment, the elf dragged him through the hedge – and there he was at the party! You should have seen the fairies, brownies, elves, gnomes, and pixies there! Hundreds of them, all chatting and laughing and dancing. When they saw the elf with the pink monkey they crowded round in surprise. The monkey blushed pinker than ever.

'I don't like being here without my tail,' he whispered to the elf. 'I don't feel dressed.'

'Don't be silly!' said the elf. 'Oh, listen, everyone, I've had an adventure! A frog stole my shawl – and I met this monkey who had a *pinned*-on tail – and he unpinned it and gave it to me for a scarf!'

'Three cheers for good old Monkey!' cried all the fairies and they swung Monkey round and round till he felt quite giddy. Nobody seemed to mind him not having a tail. The elf took it off when she danced and put it on a chair. Monkey kept his eyes on it, because he didn't want it to be lost. The next time the little elf put it round her neck, he went up to her and told her how he had meant to go to the little old woman who lived under the hedge and ask her to fix it on properly for him.

'Poor old Monkey!' said the elf, patting his big nose. 'Don't you worry about that. I know enough magic for that!'

'*Do* you!' said Monkey in surprise.

'Of course!' said the elf. 'Look – the party is

nearly over. I can borrow a shawl to go home in. You can have your tail back – and we'll fix it on properly for you – without a pin or anything.'

She clapped her hands and a dozen little folk danced up to her. She told them what she wanted, and they made a circle with the monkey in the middle. They all danced round, singing a little magic song – and then the elf threw the tail straight at monkey's back – and lo and behold, it stuck there, in exactly the right place! Fancy that!

'It's on, it's on!' shouted Monkey, tugging at

it in delight to make sure. 'Oh, thank you a hundred times, little elf.'

The elf hugged him. 'You're a darling,' she said. 'I'm pleased to have done you a good turn. I did love wearing your warm tail for a scarf. I might come and borrow it again – you never know!'

Monkey went home as happy as could be. And *how* all the toys stared when he showed them his tail and told them his adventures. He *was* proud of having a tail that had been a scarf, I can tell you!

The Princess and the Cottage-Girl

Anna often saw the little Princess Peronel walking in the woods with her nurse. She stood and watched her. Peronel was pretty. She had lovely clothes. She had a pony of her own. She had a car to go riding in. She had the most lovely food, Anna was sure.

'I don't like Peronel,' said Anna to herself. She was jealous of the little princess, and if she could have smacked her, she would.

'She's got so many things and I haven't anything at all!' thought Anna. 'I hate her!'

One day the princess came running by Anna all alone. For the first time she had no one with her. She stopped by Anna and laughed. 'What do you think?' she said. 'My nurse is asleep and I have run away and left her. Shall we have a game?'

Anna did not smile. She looked at the princess's fine clothes with envy, and then she looked down at her rough red dress.

'I don't want to play with you,' she said rudely, to Peronel. 'You've got all the luck and I haven't any! You're a princess and I am only a cottage-girl.'

'Surely you don't think I'm lucky to be a princess!' cried Peronel in surprise. 'What – lucky to have to go out always with a nurse, never alone! Lucky to have to sit for hours and hours at dull parties where there's much too much to eat and drink! Lucky to have a father and mother who are so busy being a king and queen that they haven't time to tuck me up at night!'

'Well, you don't think I'm lucky to be a poor little cottage-girl, do you?' said Anna. 'I have to mind our baby. I have to live in a poky little room, and share my bed with my little sister. I have to work in the fields with my father. I have to help my mother to bake cakes.'

'Oh, how lovely!' said Peronel. 'Our palace

cook is far too grand even to let me peep in the kitchen. I say – we're awfully alike, aren't we? Shall we change places for a bit? You be me, and I'll be you! Do!'

It wasn't a bit of good saying no to Peronel. Before Anna knew what was happening, she was in Peronel's clothes and Peronel was in hers. Peronel danced off to Anna's cottage to find the baby. She loved babies and there was none at the palace.

Peronel's nurse appeared, hot and angry. She saw Anna and thought she was the princess. 'You naughty little girl! How dare you have dry bread for tea and no cake at all!' Anna was taken off to the palace. The nurse was very, very strict, much stricter than Anna's mother. She nagged at Anna all the time. 'Elbows off

the table! Don't talk with your mouth full! What have you done to your hair? Is this the way for a princess to behave? I shall report you to the queen, your mother!'

When the queen came in to pay a hurried visit to the princess, the nurse gave her a very bad report.

'How naughty you are!' said the queen. 'Don't you know how important it is for a princess to learn all these things? Nurse, see that Peronel is made ready to attend a big party tonight – but you understand, Peronel, you mustn't eat anything except your milk pudding, because the other food would upset you.'

The nurse bathed and dressed Anna. She scolded all the time. 'Stand up straight. Now, let me see if you can curtsy nicely. Good gracious, child, you did that as if you had never curtsied in your life before!'

Anna couldn't help looking forward to the party – but oh, how dull it was! It lasted for hours, and most of the time Anna had to sit quite still, or have her hand kissed by a lot of old gentlemen she didn't like. Then, at the banquet, she was not allowed to have any of the beautiful food on the table.

'Just your milk pudding, dear,' whispered the nurse.

'I want some jelly!' said Anna loudly. The queen was shocked.

'Take her to bed,' she said. 'She must be tired.'

So Anna was hustled away, scolded, and put to bed. She cried. The queen didn't come to say goodnight. The nurse gave her a peck on the cheek and that was all. Anna was lonely.

'I don't like being a princess,' she thought. 'It isn't much fun after all. Peronel must have had a dull time. I'm going home and Peronel will have to come back.'

So she slipped out of bed and dressed. She climbed out of the window and ran through the palace grounds. She came at last to her own little cottage. She climbed up the old apple tree outside her bedroom window and tapped Peronel on the shoulder.

Peronel awoke. She was lying cuddled up to Anna's fat little sister. She sat up.

'I've come back,' said Anna. 'You dress quickly and go back to the palace.'

'I don't want to,' said Peronel at once. 'I simply love your home. I think that your mother is the nicest woman I ever knew. Do you know, she took me on her knee tonight and told me a story?'

'She always does that,' said Anna. 'Quick, get up.'

'And she came and tucked me up and kissed me goodnight,' said Peronel. 'And I do so love your little baby. I wish I could look after him all day. And your fat little sister here loves me. We are going blackberrying tomorrow. That will be fun.'

'No, you're not,' said Anna. 'Do get up.'

'Anna, your father is so nice too,' said Peronel. 'He gave me the top of his egg at teatime. My father never did that.'

'Well – my father always does,' said Anna. 'We take it in turn to have the top of his egg. Peronel, will you get up?'

'And I love your cosy kitchen,' said the little princess. 'You've no idea how warm and comfortable and homey it was this evening. A palace is never homey. Anna, I do beg and beg of you to change places with me and let me stay here with your darling mother and little baby brother and sister. Anna, do.'

'No,' said Anna. 'Get up.'

'But, Anna, you said you were jealous of me, you said I was lucky to be a princess – well, I'm telling you that you can be lucky too, if you want to,' said Peronel. 'Don't you want to be a princess?'

'No,' said Anna, 'I don't. I was silly to be jealous. I just made myself unhappy, and I hated you, when all the time you were a nice little girl I'd like to play with. It's no fun being something you weren't meant to be. I want to come back home.'

'All right,' said Peronel, with a sigh. 'I didn't really think you'd want to give up this cosy little home, with your nice mother and father. How I'd love them! Anna, will you let me come and nurse your baby some time, if I can slip away from my nurse?'

'Yes,' said Anna. 'And you can come and play with me, because I like you very much. I was silly and horrid and stupid. Jealousy is a nasty thing – it makes you see things all wrong.'

'I'm not jealous of you,' said Peronel, 'but I do think you're lucky, Anna, I do, I do. Let's be friends, shall we?'

So they are. They play together when they can, and Peronel nurses the baby as often as she is allowed to. Anna isn't jealous any more – she knows that if she is, Peronel will only be too glad to change places with her again!

The Pixies' Party

It was a very hot afternoon. Annie had taken out her two big dolls for a ride in their pram, but she hadn't gone very far because the sun was really so *very* hot. So she had sat down in the shade of the hedge, and the two dolls lay in the pram with their eyes closed, fast asleep.

Annie was nearly asleep too. She sat very still, her eyes almost closed and suddenly she felt sure that she could hear very small voices somewhere. They sounded rather like birds' voices, high and trilly – but they weren't birds.

Annie listened hard. The sound came from the other side of the hedge. The little girl turned herself quietly round and knelt down beside the thick hedge. She parted the leaves and peeped through.

And what a surprise she got! On the other side of the hedge, in the sunshine, there was a pixie party going on! Annie could hardly believe her eyes. She saw five small pixies there, sitting round a toadstool table – and a very big toadstool it was too, the biggest Annie had ever seen.

On the table was a birthday cake with five tiny candles burning on it. There were small dishes of sandwiches, buns and biscuits, and each pixie had a cup of tea. Annie looked and looked and looked.

The pixies were very merry. They laughed and talked in their bird-like voices, and seemed very happy. And then, as Annie watched, a strange thing happened. A great, prickly hedgehog came walking up and didn't seem to see the toadstool table with the pixies round it. They shouted at him but he took no notice. Right into it he went and broke the stalk of the toadstool so that the top fell off and all the cups, plates and dishes tumbled with a crash to the ground.

The clumsy hedgehog walked on quite calmly,

and disappeared into the hedge. The pixies all began to cry, when they saw their lovely tea party quite spoilt, and all their plates and dishes broken.

'My birthday party's spoilt,' wept the smallest pixie.

'Never mind,' said another. 'Don't cry. We can still eat the cakes and things. They are not spoilt.'

'But there are no plates or dishes left,' wept the little birthday pixie.

Annie felt very sorry. She suddenly remembered her new tea set at home. It was just about the same size as the pixie's. So she pressed her face through the leaves and spoke softly to the surprised little folk.

'Don't be frightened! It's only Annie, a little girl, speaking to you! I saw all that happened – and I just want to say that if you like I'll run home and get my doll's tea set for you. Then you can have your party again properly.'

The pixies stared in astonishment at the little girl. They could only see her face peeping through the hedge – but it looked such a nice, kind face that they were quite sure Annie wouldn't harm them.

'Oh, thank you!' said the smallest pixie, gratefully. 'It's so kind of you. We'd love you to lend us your tea set.'

Annie left her dolls asleep in their pram and ran off home. She found her tea set in its cardboard box and went back to the hedge with it. This time she went to the pixies' side of the hedge. She knelt down, took off the box lid and then, dear me, how delighted the little folk were to see such a very pretty little tea set!

It was of pink china with blue forget-me-nots all over it. There was a fine teapot, a milk jug,

a little sugar basin, six cups and saucers, six plates and two little cake dishes. So you see, it was a very nice set.

'The toadstool table is broken,' said Annie. 'What will you have for a table now?' 'I'll go and fetch my own table,' said one of the pixies. 'I live near here!'

She ran off into the hedge and went down what looked like a mouse hole. She soon came back carrying a neat little folding table. She set it up, and put the cloth on it. Then the pixies helped Annie to lay the table.

'You won't want the sixth cup and saucer and plate,' said Annie. 'There are only five of you.'

'No – there are *six* of us now!' said the smallest pixie. 'We want you to come to the party too, Annie. You have been so kind!'

Well, wasn't that exciting! Annie was so pleased. She laid the sixth little cup and saucer for herself. Then the pixies put back the biscuits, the cakes, the sandwiches and the birthday cake. There weren't quite enough plates for those so Annie picked some small leaves and made those do.

'Now I'll make some tea,' said the smallest pixie. To Annie's surprise she lifted up a big dock leaf growing nearby and there, underneath, was a little fire with a kettle boiling away on it! The pixie soon made a fresh pot of tea in Annie's small teapot and poured some milk into the jug from a bottle. Then she filled up the sugar basin and everything was ready.

'Now we can begin my birthday party again,'

said the little pixie, happily. 'Sit down beside me, little girl.'

So down Annie sat, and she and the five small pixies ate and drank from the doll's tea set. Annie had often played with her tea set and made pretend tea for her dolls – but she had never had a proper tea like this before. She felt most excited.

'Do you think I could pour out one cup of tea?' she asked the little pixie. 'I would so like to.'

'Of course!' said the pixie. So Annie poured a little milk into her small cup from the milk jug, put in two tiny lumps of sugar from the sugar basin, and then poured some steaming hot tea from the teapot. It was such fun.

The sandwiches were delicious, and the cakes tasted lovely. Annie was given a piece of the birthday cake too, a very big piece, and she did enjoy it. It was chocolate cream inside, and white and pink icing on the outside. The candles were all lit again and burned very well.

Just as Annie was finishing her cake she heard a bell ringing in the distance.

'Oh dear!' she said. 'That's Mummy ringing the bell for me to go in to tea. Goodness, I shan't want any tea at all now I've had such a lovely one with you!'

'We'll wash up all the dishes,' said the smallest pixie, 'and we'll leave the box with the tea things in, at the bottom of your garden tonight. You'll find it there tomorrow morning. Thank you so much for being so kind.'

'Thank *you* very much for asking me to your birthday party!' cried Annie, getting up. 'Good-bye!'

She squeezed through the hedge, found her dolls' pram, and wheeled it home quickly, thinking joyfully about the lovely tea party she had been to. When she got home her

mother called to her.

'Hurry up, Annie, you *have* been a long time! Tea is waiting.'

'I don't think I want any, Mummy,' said Annie. 'I've been to a birthday party!'

'Don't talk nonsense!' said her mother. 'Go and wash your hands and then sit down quickly.'

Annie washed her hands, and then told her mother all about the pixie's party. But her mother only laughed and said: 'You fell asleep in the hot sun, Annie dear, and dreamed it all. Go and look in your toy cupboard and I'm sure you'll find your tea set there.'

Annie went to look – but it wasn't there of course. 'The pixies said they were going to wash everything and put my tea set back in the garden tonight,' she said.

'Well, if they do, I'll believe you!' said her mother.

So, just before it got dark, Annie went out to look in the garden – and there, carefully placed on the little table in the summerhouse, was her tea set box! She opened the lid and found her tea set inside, all clean, washed most beautifully, and each cup and dish arranged in its own place.

'There you are, Mummy!' cried Annie, running indoors. 'Here's my tea set come back again, all washed, just as I said. So you see I was right!'

'Dear me, how funny!' said her mother, in astonishment. 'Well, I do believe you now, Annie. What an adventure you had! I wish I had been at that birthday party too!'

So do I – don't you?

The Most Surprising Chair

O nce there was a lazy child called Susan. She wouldn't get up in the morning, she wouldn't hurry herself to dress, and even in the daytime she would flop down into an armchair and stay there till her mother tipped her out.

She was always late for morning school, and her teacher scolded her hard. But when she began to be late for afternoon school as well, her teacher wondered whatever was the matter.

'Well, you see,' explained Susan, 'I do feel so sleepy after my dinner that I curl up in an arm-chair and fall asleep. When I wake up I'm late. My mother won't bother about me any more, so I'm afraid I shall always be late!'

Now the armchair that Susan curled up in after her dinner was an old, old one. It loved people to sit in it, and it was good to old people and made itself as comfy as possible for them.

But it really couldn't bear lazy people, and when Susan, who was young and strong, curled up in it so lazily every day, the old chair grumbled away to itself and tried to make its seat as hard and as uncomfortable as it could.

But it wasn't a bit of use. Susan didn't even notice it was hard. She went off to sleep at

once! She always ate too much at dinner time and this made her very sleepy.

The chair creaked loudly. Susan didn't wake. The chair made its seat as hard as wood and its arms like iron. Susan didn't stir. The school bell rang loudly. Susan slept peacefully on. And this happened every afternoon. Wasn't it dreadful!

Susan's mother was so tired of scolding her that she no longer bothered to wake her up.

'You can be punished for your lazy ways at school,' she said. 'I can't be bothered with you any more.'

But the old chair grew more and more angry. It worked itself up to such a state that one afternoon a most peculiar thing happened.

Susan had eaten a big plate of meat pie and had had three helpings of treacle pudding. She felt very sleepy as usual, and curled up in the old chair. She fell asleep and even snored a little.

This was too much for the chair. It gave an angry creak and then another. It shook itself. It lifted up a foot and tapped loudly on the floor!

Susan slept on! The chair tapped with another foot. Susan snored gently. Oh, naughty Susan, wake up, before anything happens!

The chair lost its temper.

'I've four feet and four legs. I can walk on them as well as stand on them. I'll take this lazy child to school and see what she says when she wakes up there!'

And with that the chair lifted up first one leg, then another – and soon it was walking out of the room, making a clip-clop noise on the floor as it went.

Susan slept peacefully on. The chair went into the hall. The front door was open, and the postman was just putting a letter on the mat. He saw the chair, gave a frightened shout and rushed off! The chair gave a creak and went out of the front door.

Well, as soon as it was in the street, with people walking near, everyone stopped in surprise. They stared at the chair, they nudged one another when they saw the sleeping Susan, and they looked half frightened. But nobody tried to stop the chair until it met Mr Plod the policeman.

He saw the chair coming towards him and looked most astonished. When it came near him, making a clip-clop noise with its feet on the pavement, he cleared his throat politely – 'er-hurrrrrr!' – and put up his hand.

92

'Stop!' he said. But the chair took no notice at all. It just gave a loud and rather rude creak, and went under the policeman's hand. Mr Plod was annoyed. He took out his notebook and ran after the chair.

'Are you a new kind of motorcar?' he cried. 'Where's your licence? You haven't got a numberplate!'

The chair creaked again and set off so fast that the policeman was soon left behind. It bumped into Mrs Hurry and gave her a dreadful shock. It trod on Mr Toppy's foot and made him hop about in pain, and he shouted in surprise to see such a curious sight as an armchair hurrying by with a little girl fast asleep in it.

At last the armchair reached the school. The children had all gone in, but the door was still a little open. The teacher was calling the children's names to see that they were all in time.

'Alice! Ben! Mary! Mollie! Eric!'

'Here, Miss Brown. Here, Miss Brown,' answered the children politely, as their names were called.

And then Miss Brown came to Susan's name. 'Susan!' she called – and at that very moment the door opened and in came the armchair with Susan!

'Look! Look!' shrieked all the children. 'Susan's in time – the chair has brought her! She's fast asleep – oh, she's fast asleep!'

They all began to laugh loudly as they gathered round the creaking armchair, which was not standing still by Miss Brown's desk.

Susan awoke, for the noise was really almost deafening. She rubbed her eyes and looked around.

'Oh!' she said. 'Where am I? I've been asleep! How did I come to school?'

'The armchair brought you, the armchair brought you!' shouted the children, dancing round in delight. 'It was awake, and it brought you by itself! Oh, what a funny thing, Susan!'

Susan was ashamed. She got out of the armchair and ran to her desk. She sat down, very red.

When the chair saw Susan safely at her desk it gave a creak as if to say goodbye, and clip-clopped to the door. It squeezed out and clip-clopped home, taking no notice of any one. Susan had got to school in time for once!

Well, do you know, Susan got teased so much about the chair bringing her to school, and was so afraid that perhaps her bed might play her the same trick in the morning, that she quite turned over a new leaf. Now she is up as soon as her mother calls her, and she never dares to go to sleep after dinner.

So she isn't late for school any more and has got as many good marks as any one. But if the chair sees her yawning, you should hear it creak!

'Cr-eeeeeeeeak!' And Susan stops yawning at once and gets some work to do. Poor old Susan! She never sits in that old armchair any more, as you can guess!

Mr Noodle's Eggs

Mr Noodle was very pleased with his hens one market day, because they had laid him fifty-three eggs. Nice brown eggs they were, too, just the right sort for breakfast.

'Fifty-three!' said Mr Noodle to himself, as he carried them to market in a big round basket. 'Fifty-three! And eggs are ten pence each today. Fifty-three tenpences – now what does that come to?'

He worked it out in his head, and found that if he sold all his eggs he would have five pounds and thirty pence in his pocket. What a lot of money!

Mr Noodle got to the market and put his big

basket of eggs down on the roadway. He stood in front of them, and called out the price of his eggs to the passers-by.

'Brown eggs, ten pence each! Brown eggs for sale!'

Presently he began to think what he would do with the five pounds and thirty pence, and he decided that he would buy a goose and sit her on some goose eggs. Then, when all the goslings hatched out, he would sell them and make a lot more money. Oh!

Mr Noodle smiled so broadly when he thought of his geese that Mrs Twinkle and Mr Tot, who were nearby, wondered what the matter was. So they asked him.

'I'm just thinking how rich I shall be one day,' said Mr Noodle. 'I'm going to buy some goose eggs and a goose to sit on them when I've sold all these eggs laid by my hens. When the goslings hatch out, I shall fatten them up and sell them for fifty pence each.'

'You won't be very rich,' said Mrs Twinkle. 'As likely as not your goose eggs will be bad.'

'Indeed they won't,' said Mr Noodle, so crossly that Dame Humpy and Farmer Barley-corn came up to see what he was talking about. 'My goose eggs will be good ones. Well,

I shall make about six pounds out of the goslings, and with that I shall buy a goat! Ha, ha, you'll stare when I have a goat of my own!'

'What good will a goat do you?' said Farmer Barley-corn, with a laugh. 'You won't make much out of a goat.'

'Won't I?' cried Mr Noodle, dancing about in excitement, and making quite a crowd come round him. 'Won't I? I tell you I'll make gold out of my goat, for I'll sell its milk to Mrs Welcome at the Big House for her three children, and I'll soon make so much money by it that I'll be able to buy a cow. Ho, ho!'

'Silly man,' said Mr Tot. 'It will take you

years to save up for a cow. You don't know what you are talking about.'

'Yes I do, yes I do!' cried Mr Noodle. 'I can buy a good cow cheap from my old uncle over the hill. Ha! And when I have a cow and sell its good, creamy milk, I shall make my fortune! I shall put away all the money I get, and then, one day, I shall take it out, put it into a bag, and go to buy a fine new house. I'll have it built on the hill over there, where you can all see it.'

'Pooh!' said Farmer Barley-corn. 'You think you'll be very grand, don't you, Noodle? Well, you won't. You'll be just the same silly old Noodle you've always been.'

'I shan't, I shan't!' yelled Mr Noodle, in a fine temper. 'I shall be a wise, grand, rich man, and you'll be proud to know me. But shall I know *you*? No, I shan't! I won't bother myself then with Farmer Barley-corns or Dame Humpys or Mrs Twinkles. No, I shall go calling on My Lady This and My Lord That, and you will all stand and look at me when my carriage goes rolling by.'

'That certainly would be a fine sight to see,' said Mr Tot, laughing loudly. 'Mr Noodle riding in his own carriage! My, what a joke!'

Mr Noodle frowned angrily. 'Yes,' he said, 'you may laugh if you like. But you won't laugh then. No! I'll say to my coachman: "Do you see those silly people standing there staring? Well, take your whip and send them away!" Ha! Then you'll run like this – and like this – and like this!'

Mr Noodle ran backwards, pretending to be frightened of his coachman's whip. He dodged here and dodged there – and, oh, my goodness, whatever do you think? He didn't see where he was going and he fell right into his basket of eggs! Crash! Splash! A score of yellow jets gushed up from the basket and poor Mr Noodle sat there

in astonishment and dismay.

'Oh, my eggs, my eggs!' he wailed, trying to get up. But the basket stuck to him, and the poor man had to walk about asking someone to pull it off. Farmer Barley-corn gave it a tug, and off it came with all the smashed eggs.

Mr Noodle looked sorrowfully at the yellow basket, and shook his head.

'I'm a noodle,' he said, 'there's no doubt about it. Just a silly big noodle. Look at my lovely eggs – all gone, and with them go my goslings, my goat, my cow, my new house, my carriage, and everything! Well, well, Noodle by name, and noodle by nature, I suppose!'

And off he went home carrying his eggy basket, wondering what to say to Mrs Noodle. When she heard his story she was very angry. She chased him out of the kitchen with a broom, and the poor man had to spend the night sitting in the henhouse with the hens. Ah me!

A Puddle for the Donkeys

One day Dame Bonnet set out to catch the bus to the market. And, at the same time, Dame Two-Shoes set out to get the bus, too. They met on the common that leads down to where the big green bus stops three times a day.

'Good day to you, Dame Bonnet,' said Dame Two-Shoes. 'And where are you off to this fine morning?'

'To the market to buy me a good fat donkey,' said Dame Bonnet.

'What a strange thing!' said Dame Two-Shoes. 'I'm going to market to buy the very same thing.'

'Well, well, there will be plenty of good fat donkeys for sale,' said Dame Bonnet. 'Will you ride home on yours?'

'That I will,' said Dame Two-Shoes. 'I'm taking the morning's bus there, but I'm riding home on my own donkey, so I am.'

'And that's what I shall do, too,' said Dame Bonnet. 'I'm taking a carrot for my good donkey. Look!'

'Well, well, how do we think alike!' said Dame Two-Shoes, and she held out a large carrot, too. 'I've got a carrot as well.'

'I expect our donkeys will be thirsty this hot day,' said Dame Bonnet, looking round. 'There's a nice big puddle near here, left by the rain. I mean to let my donkey drink it up.'

The two old dames looked at the puddle of water. 'I had that idea, too,' said Dame Two-Shoes, frowning. 'That puddle is only enough for one donkey. You must let mine share it, or mine will have none. Let them have half each. That will be fair.'

'If my donkey is here first, he shall have all the puddle,' said Dame Bonnet at once. 'I spoke about it first.'

'Don't be so mean,' cried Dame Two-Shoes. 'Would you have my donkey die of thirst?'

'Well, I shall not let mine die of thirst, either,' said Dame Bonnet. 'I don't care about yours. I have to think of my own good fat donkey. I don't go to market to buy donkeys and then let them die of thirst on the way home. The puddle is for my own donkey. So make up your mind about that!'

The old horse who lived on the common came wandering by, wondering why the old dames were talking so loudly. He saw the gleaming puddle of water and went over to it.

'Now look here!' said Dame Two-Shoes, angrily. 'For the last time, Dame Bonnet, will you let my donkey share that puddle? For the last time I ask you.'

'And for the last time I say that I shall look after my own good fat donkey, and not yours,' said Dame Bonnet, in a rage.

Then they heard the sound of gulping, and they turned to see what it was. It was the old horse drinking up every scrap of the puddle. There wasn't a drop left at all.

'Look at that!' cried Dame Two-Shoes in a fine old temper. 'That greedy horse has been drinking up our donkeys' puddle! You bad horse!'

'Who do you belong to?' said Dame Bonnet. 'I'll go and tell your master. That puddle belonged to our two good fat donkeys. Now, when we ride them home tonight, there will be no puddle for them to drink and they will both die of thirst.'

'Hrrrumph!' said the horse, and backed away in alarm.

There came the sound of rumbling wheels and the old dames looked down to the road at the bottom of the common.

'The bus, it's the bus!' they cried. 'It's coming! Hurry, hurry! We shall never get to the market in time!'

So off they ran over the common path, the old horse looking after them in astonishment. How they ran! They panted and they puffed, they pulled their skirts away from the prickly gorse bushes and tried to hold them, they skipped over the rabbit holes, and ran like two-year-olds.

The bus stopped. Nobody got out. Nobody got in. The driver looked round, but didn't see Dame Bonnet and Dame Two-Shoes scurrying along.

They had no breath left to shout at him. They ran and ran. But the bus went off without them, down the country road, out of sight.

'Oh!' said Dame Bonnet, almost in tears. 'Now we can't get to the market in time.'

'We can't buy our donkeys,' said Dame Two-Shoes. 'We shall have to walk home,' said Dame Bonnet.

'If we hadn't quarrelled about the pool of water that isn't there, we should be halfway to market now, we should buy good fat donkeys, and we should ride home on them,' wept Dame Two-Shoes.

'And we would have given them a drink before we started so that they wouldn't have wanted the puddle at all,' said Dame Bonnet.

They went slowly back home again. The old horse saw them and stared after them.

'Now what do they want with donkeys?' he said to himself. 'Donkeys themselves, that's what they are! Hrrrumph!'

And I rather think he was right.

The Wizard's Umbrella

Ribby the Gnome lived in a small cottage at the end of Tiptoe Village. Nobody liked him because he was always borrowing things and never bringing them back! It was most annoying of him.

The things he borrowed most were umbrellas. I really couldn't tell you how many umbrellas Ribby had borrowed in his life – hundreds, I should think! He had borrowed Dame Twinkle's nice red one, he had taken Mr Biscuit the Baker's old green one, he had had Pixie Dimple's little grey and pink sunshade, and many, many more.

If people came to ask for them back, he

would hunt all about and then say he was very sorry but he must have lent their umbrellas to someone else – he certainly hadn't got them in his cottage now. And no one would ever know what had happened to their nice umbrellas!

Of course, Ribby the Gnome knew quite well where they were! They were all tied up tightly together hidden in his loft. And once a month, Ribby would set out on a dark night, when nobody was about, and take with him all the borrowed umbrellas. He would go to the town of Here-We-Are, a good many miles away, and then the next day he would go through the streets there, crying: 'Umbrellas for sale! Fine umbrellas!'

He would sell the whole bundle, and make quite a lot of money. Then the wicked gnome would buy himself some fine new clothes, and perhaps a new chair or some new curtains for his cottage and go home again.

Now one day it happened that Dame Twinkle went over to the town of Here-We-Are, and paid a call on her cousin, Mother Tantrums. And there standing in the umbrella stand in Mother Tantrums' hall, Dame Twinkle saw her very own nice red umbrella, that she had lent to Ribby the Gnome the month before!

She stared at it in great surprise. However did it come to be in her cousin's umbrella stand? Surely she hadn't lent it to Mother Tantrums? No, no – she was certain, quite certain, she had lent it to Ribby the Gnome.

'What are you staring at?' asked Mother Tantrums in surprise.

'Well,' said Dame Twinkle, pointing to the red umbrella, 'it's a funny thing, Cousin Tantrums, but, you know, that's my red umbrella you've got in your umbrella stand.'

'Nonsense!' said Mother Tantrums. 'Why, that's an umbrella I bought for a pound from a little gnome who often comes round selling things.'

'A *pound*!' cried Dame Twinkle in horror. 'My goodness, gracious me, I paid seven pounds and fifty pence for it! A pound, indeed! What next!'

'What are you talking about?' asked Mother Tantrums, quite cross. 'It's *my* umbrella, not yours – and a very good bargain it was, too!'

'I should think so!' said Dame Twinkle, looking lovingly at the red umbrella, which she had been very fond of indeed. 'Tell me, Cousin, what sort of a gnome was this that sold you your umbrella?'

'Oh, he was short and rather fat,' said Mother Tantrums.

'Lots of gnomes are short and fat,' said Dame Twinkle. 'Can't you remember anything else about him?'

'Well, he wore a bright yellow scarf round his neck,' said Mother Tantrums, 'and his eyes were a very light green.'

'That's Ribby the Gnome!' cried Dame Twinkle, quite certain. 'He always wears a yellow scarf, and his eyes are a very funny green. Oh, the wicked scamp! I suppose he borrows our umbrellas in order to sell them when he can! Oh, the horrid little thief! I shall tell the wizard who lives in our village and ask him to punish Ribby. Yes, I will! He deserves a very nasty punishment indeed!'

So when she went back to Tiptoe Village, Dame Twinkle went to call on the Wizard Deep-One. He was a great friend of hers, and when he heard about Ribby's wickedness he shook his head in horror.

'He must certainly be punished,' said the wizard, nodding his head. 'Leave it to me, Dame Twinkle. I will see to it.'

Deep-One thought for a long time, and then he smiled. Ha, he would lay a little trap for Ribby that would teach him never to borrow umbrellas again. He took a spell and with it he made a very fine umbrella indeed. It was deep blue, and for a handle it had a dog's head. It was really a marvellous umbrella.

The wizard put it into his umbrella stand and then left his front door open wide every day so that anyone passing by could see the dog's-head umbrella quite well. He was sure that Ribby the Gnome would spy it the very first time he came walking by.

When Ribby did see the umbrella he stopped to have a good look at it. My, what a lovely umbrella! He hadn't noticed it before, so it must be a new one. See the dog's head on it, it looked almost real! Oh, if Ribby could only get *that* umbrella, he could sell it for a good many pounds in the town of Here-We-Are. He was sure that the enchanter who lived there would be very pleased to buy it.

'Somehow or other I must get that umbrella,' thought Ribby.

'The very next time it rains I will hurry by the wizard's house, and pop in and ask him to lend it to me! I don't expect he will, but I'll ask, anyway!'

So on the following Thursday, when a rain-storm came, Ribby hurried out of his cottage without an umbrella and ran to Deep-One's house. The front door was wide open as usual and Ribby could quite well see the dog-headed umbrella in the hall stand. He ran up the path, and knocked at the open door.

'Who's there?' came the wizard's voice.

'It's me, Ribby the Gnome!' said the gnome. 'Please, Wizard Deep-One, could you lend me an umbrella? It's pouring with rain and I am getting so wet. I am sure I shall get a dreadful cold if someone doesn't lend me an umbrella.'

'Dear, dear, dear!' said the wizard, coming out of his parlour, and looking at the wet gnome. 'You certainly are *very* wet! Yes, I will lend you an umbrella – but mind, Ribby, let me warn you to bring it back tomorrow in case something unpleasant happens to you.'

'Oh, of course, of course,' said Ribby. 'I always return things I borrow, Wizard. You shall have it back tomorrow as sure as eggs are eggs.'

'Well, take that one from the hall stand, Ribby,' said the wizard, pointing to the dog's-head umbrella. Ribby took it in delight. He had got what he wanted. How easy it had been after all! He, ho, he wouldn't bring it back tomorrow, not he! He would take it to the town of Here-We-Are as soon as ever he could and sell it to the enchanter there. What luck!

He opened it, said thank you to the smiling wizard, and rushed down the path with the blue umbrella. He was half afraid the wizard would call him back – but no, Deep-One let him go without a word – but he chuckled very deeply as he saw the gnome vanishing round the corner. How easily Ribby had fallen into the trap!

Of course Ribby didn't take the umbrella back next day. No, he put it up in his loft and didn't go near the wizard's house at all. If he saw the wizard in the street he would pop into a shop until he had gone by. He wasn't going to let him have his umbrella back for a moment!

Now after three weeks had gone by, and Ribby had heard nothing from the wizard about his umbrella, he decided it would be safe to go to Here-We-Are and sell it.

'I expect the wizard had forgotten all about it by now,' thought Ribby. 'He is very forgetful.'

So that night Ribby packed up three other umbrellas, and tied the wizard's dog-headed one to them very carefully. Then he put the bundle over his shoulder and set out in the darkness. Before morning came he was in the town of Here-We-Are, and the folk there heard him crying out his wares in a loud voice.

'Umbrellas for sale! Fine umbrellas for sale! Come and buy!'

Ribby easily sold the other three umbrellas he had with him and then he made his way to the enchanter's house. The dog-headed umbrella was now the only one left.

The enchanter came to the door and looked at the umbrella that Ribby showed him. But as soon as his eye fell on it he drew back in horror.

'Buy that umbrella!' he cried. 'Not I! Why, it's alive!'

'Alive!' said Ribby, laughing scornfully. 'No, sir, it is as dead as a doornail!'

'I tell you, that umbrella is *alive*!' said the enchanter and he slammed the door in the astonished gnome's face.

Ribby looked at the dog-headed umbrella, feeling very much puzzled – and as he looked, a very odd feeling came over him. The dog's head really did look alive. It wagged one ear as Ribby looked at it, and then it showed its teeth at the gnome and growled fiercely!

My goodness! Ribby was frightened almost out of his life! He dropped the umbrella on to the ground and fled away as fast as his fat little legs would carry him!

As soon as the umbrella touched the ground a very peculiar thing happened to it. It grew four legs, and the head became bigger. The body was made of the long umbrella part, and the tail was the end bit. It could even wag!

'Oh, oh, an umbrella-dog!' cried all the people of Here-We-Are town and they fled away in fright. But the strange dog took no notice of anyone but Ribby the Gnome. He galloped after him, barking loudly.

He did look queer. His umbrella-body flapped as he went along on his stout little doggy legs, and his tongue hung out of his mouth. It was most astonishing. People looked out of their windows at it, and everyone closed their front doors with a bang in case the strange umbrella-dog should come running into their houses.

Ribby was dreadfully frightened. He ran on and on, and every now and then he looked round.

'Oh, my goodness, that umbrella-dog's still

after me!' he panted. 'What shall I do? Oh, why, why, why did I borrow the wizard's umbrella? Why didn't I take it back? I might have known there would be something peculiar about it!'

119

The umbrella-dog raced on, and came so near to Ribby that it was able to snap at his twinkling legs. Snap! The dog's sharp teeth took a piece out of Ribby's green trousers!

'Ow! Ooh! Ow!' shrieked Ribby in horror, and he shot on twice as fast, panting like a railway train going up a hill! Everybody watched from their windows and some of them

laughed because it was really a very peculiar sight.

Ribby looked out for someone to open a door so that he could run in. But every single door was shut. He must just run on and on. But how much longer could he run? He was getting terribly out of breath.

The umbrella-dog was enjoying himself very much. Ho, this was better fun than being a dull old umbrella! This was seeing life! If only he could catch that nasty little running thing in front, what fun he would have!

The umbrella-dog ran a bit faster and caught up Ribby once more. This time he jumped up and bit a piece out of the gnome's lovely yellow scarf. Then he jumped again and nipped a tiny piece out of Ribby's leg.

'OW!' yelled Ribby, jumping high into the air. 'OW! You horrid cruel dog! Leave me alone! How dare you, I say? Wait till I get home!'

The dog sat down to chew the piece he had bitten out of Ribby's yellow scarf, and the gnome ran on, hoping that the dog would forget about him.

'Oh, if only I could get home!' cried the panting gnome. 'Once I'm in my house I'm safe!'

He ran on and on, through the wood and over the common that lay between the town of Here-We-Are and the village of Tiptoe. The dog did not seem to be following him. Ribby kept looking round but there was no umbrella-dog there. If only he could get home in time!

Just as he got to Tiptoe Village he heard a pattering of feet behind him. He looked round and saw the umbrella-dog just behind him. Oh, what a shock for poor Ribby!

'Look, look!' cried everyone in surprise. 'There's a mad umbrella-dog after Ribby. Run, Ribby, run!'

Poor Ribby had to run all through the village of Tiptoe to get to his cottage. The dog ran at his heels snapping every now and again, making the gnome leap high into the air with pain and fright.

'I'll never, never, never borrow an umbrella again, or anything else!' vowed the gnome, as the dog nipped his heel with his sharp teeth. 'Oh, why didn't I take the wizard's umbrella back?'

At last he was home. He rushed up the path, pushed the door open and slammed it. But, alas, the umbrella-dog had slipped in with him, and there it was in front of Ribby, sitting up and begging.

'OH, you horror!' shouted Ribby, trying to open the door and get out again. But the dog wouldn't let him. Every time Ribby put his hand on the handle of the door it jumped up and nipped him. So at last he stopped trying to open it and looked in despair at the strange dog, who was now sitting up and begging.

'Do you want something to eat?' said the gnome. 'Goodness, I shouldn't have thought an umbrella-dog could be hungry. Wait a bit. I've a nice joint of meat here, you shall have that, if only you will stop snapping at me!'

The dog ran by Ribby as he went hurriedly to his larder and opened the door. He took a joint of meat from a dish and gave it to the dog, who crunched it up hungrily.

Then began a very sorrowful time for Ribby! The dog wouldn't leave him for a moment and the gnome had never in his life known such a

hungry creature. Although its body was simply an umbrella, it ate and ate and ate. Ribby spent all his money on food for it, and in the days that came, often went hungry himself. The dog wouldn't leave his side, and when the gnome went out shopping the strange creature always went with him, much to the surprise and amusement of all the people in the village.

'Look!' they would cry. 'Look! There goes Ribby the gnome and his strange umbrella-dog! Where did he get it from? Why does he keep such a strange, hungry creature?'

If Ribby tried to creep off at night, or run away from the dog, it would at once start snapping and snarling at his heels, and after it had nibbled a bit out of his leg once or twice and bitten a large hole in his best coat, Ribby gave up trying to go away.

'But what shall I do?' wondered the little gnome, each night, as he looked at his empty larder. 'This dog is eating everything I have. I shall soon have no money left to buy anything.'

Ribby had had such a shock when the stolen umbrella had turned into the strange umbrella-dog, that he had never once thought of borrowing anything else. He felt much too much afraid that what he borrowed would turn into something like the dog, and he really couldn't bear that!

'I suppose I'd better get some work to do,' he

said to himself at last. 'But who will give me a job? Nobody likes me because I have always borrowed things and never taken them back. Oh dear, how foolish and stupid I have been.'

Then at last he thought he had better go to the Wizard Deep-One and confess to him all that had happened. Perhaps Deep-One would take away the horrid umbrella-dog and then Ribby would feel happier. So off he went to the wizard's house.

The wizard opened the door himself and when he saw Ribby with the dog he began to laugh. How he laughed! He held his sides and roared till the tears ran down his cheeks.

'What's the matter?' asked Ribby, in surprise. 'What is the joke?'

'*You are!*' cried the wizard, laughing more than ever. 'Ho, ho, Ribby, little did you think that I had made that dog-headed umbrella

especially for you to borrow and that I knew exactly what was going to happen! Well, you can't say that I didn't warn you. My only surprise is that you haven't come to me before for help. You can't have liked having such a strange umbrella-dog living with you, eating all your food, and snapping at your heels every moment! But it's a good punishment for you – you won't borrow things and not bring them back again, I'm sure!'

'I never, never will,' said Ribby, going very red. 'I am very sorry for all the wrong things I have done. Perhaps I had better keep this umbrella-dog to remind me to be honest, Wizard.'

'No, I'll have it,' said Deep-one. 'It will do to guard my house for me. I think any burglar would run for miles if he suddenly saw the umbrella-dog coming for him. And what are *you* going to do, Ribby? Have you any work?'

'No,' said Ribby, sorrowfully. 'Nobody likes me and I'm sure no one will give me any work to do in case I borrow something and don't return it, just as I used to do.'

'Well, well, well,' said the wizard, and his wrinkled eyes looked kindly at the sad little gnome. 'You have learned your lesson, Ribby, I can see. Come and be my gardener and grow my vegetables. I shall work you hard, but I shall pay you well, and I think you will be happy.'

So Ribby is now Deep-One's gardener, and he works hard from morning to night. But he is happy because everyone likes him now – and as for the umbrella-dog, he is as fond of Ribby as anyone else is and keeps at his heels all the time. And the funny thing is that Ribby likes him there!